The Clock Spell

by Liza Charlesworth

illustrated by Rachel Moss

ISBN: 979-8-225-02076-7

Publisher: Tara Welty
Creative Director: Tannaz Fassihi; Designer: Cynthia Ng

1 2 3 4 5 6 7 8 9 10 68 34 33 32 31 30 29 28 27 26 25

Made in Jiaxing City, China. First printing, August 2025.

SCHOLASTIC

Hello, reader! My name is Glen Gleeson.
I like to write and bake and play soccer.
Most of all, I like to relax with my pet cat.
His name is Wizard and I think he's magic.
Are you in the mood to hear a VERY spooky
thing that happened to me last night?
Good! I will tell you about the clock spell.

Well, it all started right after sunset. The dusty, old clock in our hall chimed loudly eight times: *Chime, Chime, Chime, Chime, Chime, Chime, Chime, Chime!* Those eight chimes told me it was 8 p.m., which just happens to be my very favorite hour of the whole day.

“Why is it my very favorite hour?” you ask. Well, I can explain. At 8 p.m. each night, my homework is all complete. YIPPEE! Plus, my dad always hands me a plate with a yummy, fresh-baked snack on it. Last night, it was oatmeal cookies.

After my fresh-baked snack, it is time for another treat. I get to brush my teeth with my purple electric toothbrush. Not only does my electric toothbrush make my teeth snowy white, it also plays tunes by the latest pop stars.

Do you want to know what happens next?
I get in my flannel PJs and dive into bed.
After that, Mom sits down and reads me a
chapter of a cool book like *Benny Botter*.
Then just before the clock strikes nine,
I go right to sleep with Wizard at my feet.
But that is NOT how it went last night.

Last night, when Mom left my room. . .
I was STILL wide awake. And I felt so
good that I whispered to Wizard:
"Pssssst. The last hour was wonderful!
I wish that I could do it all over again."
Then my cat swished his fluffy, black tail
and what did I hear? The old, dusty clock
chimed eight times, NOT nine: *Chime, Chime,
Chime, Chime, Chime, Chime, Chime, Chime!*

After that, things got quite nutty. ZIP, ZAP! I found myself standing back in front of that dusty, old clock and the time said 8 o'clock. Then my dad yelled out from the kitchen, "Glen, time to eat your fresh-baked snack!" Was I about to turn down a second plate of oatmeal cookies? No way. *Munch, crunch!*

I thanked my dad for the yummy cookies. "Glad you liked them," he said. "It is now 8:15. Don't you think you should brush your teeth?"

"Oh, yes!" I replied. "I'm so happy you asked." The only thing better than brushing my teeth one time with my purple electric toothbrush is brushing them twice! *Buzz, buzz, pop tunes!*

But wait. There is more for me to tell.
After my teeth were bright and clean,
my mom yelled from my room, “It’s time
to hop in bed. I’ll read you *Benny Botter*.”
“OK. That sounds fantastic!” I replied.
There was just one itty-bitty problem:
It was the SAME chapter as before.

Got it? Good. Because things got even odder.
As soon as my mom turned out the light,
that dusty, old clock in the hall chimed
eight times again: *Chime, Chime, Chime,*
Chime, Chime, Chime, Chime, Chime!
Then—*ZIP, ZAP!* Dad gave me a new plate
of fresh-baked oatmeal cookies. OK, I ate them.
But this time, my tummy hurt. . .A LOT.

After that, I brushed my teeth a third time.
Buzz, buzz, plus more silly pop tunes!
I must admit that the thrill of using my electric toothbrush was getting a bit old.
And when I hopped into my bed—Yikes!
I had to listen to Mom read the exact same chapter of *Benny Botter* yet again.
Even the best book is boring a third time!

When my mom left my room. . .I snapped.
"Pssssst. I can't take it!" I whispered to Wizard.
"I made a wish for it to be the hour of 8 p.m. forever. But that was such a mistake!
I'm sick of oatmeal cookies and my dumb electric toothbrush. Plus, it's NOT at all fun to hear the same chapter of *Benny Botter* again and again and again!"

"I wish for 24 hours in a day—not just one! This darn spell has got to end!" I cried. What happened next? OK, I will tell you. Wizard swished his fluffy, black tail and what did I hear? The dusty, old clock chimed nine times: *Chime, Chime, Chime, Chime, Chime, Chime, Chime, Chime, Chime!*

Did that mean the clock spell was broken? Was it really 9 p.m. and not 8 p.m. again? I didn't know until my dad peeked into my room and said, "It's getting late. Stop chatting with the cat and sleep. You need to wake up at 7 a.m. Then, after school, you can help me make peanut-butter cookies. Sound good?"

"That sounds VERY, VERY good!" I replied.

Dad said I needed to wake up at 7 a.m.
Plus, tomorrow we'd bake fresh cookies,
but NOT oatmeal. YIPPEE, YAHOO!
At last, the darn clock spell was broken.
I gave my cat a hug and said, "No more
wishes for me. I like 24 hours in my day!"
What did Wizard do? He purred and smiled.